Pinkalicious
Message in a Bottle

marks
the spot
in Pinkville

To Luna
—V.K.

The author gratefully acknowledges
the artistic and editorial contributions of
Daniel Griffo and Jacqueline Resnick.

I Can Read® and I Can Read Book® are trademarks of HarperCollins Publishers.

Pinkalicious: Message in a Bottle
Copyright © 2022 by VBK, Co.

PINKALICIOUS and all related logos and characters are trademarks of Victoria Kann. Used with permission.

Based on the HarperCollins book *Pinkalicious* written by
Victoria Kann and Elizabeth Kann, illustrated by Victoria Kann
All rights reserved. Printed in the United States of America.
No part of this book may be used or reproduced in any manner whatsoever without
written permission except in the case of brief quotations embodied in critical articles and reviews.
For information address HarperCollins Children's Books, a division of HarperCollins Publishers,
195 Broadway, New York, NY 10007.
www.icanread.com

Library of Congress Control Number: 2021945755
ISBN 978-0-06-300382-8 (trade bdg.)—ISBN 978-0-06-300381-1 (pbk.)

22 23 24 25 26 CWM 10 9 8 7 6 5 4 3 2
❖
First Edition

Dear Parent:

Your child's love of reading starts here!

Every child learns to read in a different way and at his or her own speed. Some go back and forth between reading levels and read favorite books again and again. Others read through each level in order. You can help your young reader improve and become more confident by encouraging his or her own interests and abilities. From books your child reads with you to the first books he or she reads alone, there are I Can Read Books for every stage of reading:

SHARED READING
Basic language, word repetition, and whimsical illustrations, ideal for sharing with your emergent reader

BEGINNING READING
Short sentences, familiar words, and simple concepts for children eager to read on their own

READING WITH HELP
Engaging stories, longer sentences, and language play for developing readers

READING ALONE
Complex plots, challenging vocabulary, and high-interest topics for the independent reader

I Can Read Books have introduced children to the joy of reading since 1957. Featuring award-winning authors and illustrators and a fabulous cast of beloved characters, I Can Read Books set the standard for beginning readers.

A lifetime of discovery begins with the magical words "I Can Read!"

Visit www.icanread.com for information
on enriching your child's reading experience.

I Can Read!

2 READING WITH HELP

Pinkalicious
Message in a Bottle

by Victoria Kann

HARPER

An Imprint of HarperCollinsPublishers

Molly and I were building
a sandcastle at the beach.
Suddenly I saw something
shimmer under the sand.

"I spy buried treasure!" I said.

"Let's dig for it," Molly said.

I shoveled and Molly scooped.

"I got it!" Molly said at last.

"It's a . . . bottle?"

"That's not just any bottle!" I said.

"It's a message in a bottle!

I've read about them.

People used to throw bottles

into the ocean to send messages."

"Wow," Molly said.

"I can't believe we found one!"

"Let's read the message!" I said.

"The top is stuck," Molly said.

I yanked and tugged.

Suddenly the top popped off.

I flew backward into the sand.

"Got it," I said with a giggle.

We carefully unrolled the paper.

I read the message out loud.

The prize goes
to the one who knows
where little Rose grows.

"It's a riddle!" Molly said.

We studied the note together.

"If we find the little rose,

it will lead us to a prize," I said.

"We have to solve the mystery!"

"I spot our first clue," Molly said.

She pointed to the back of the paper.

There was a picture of a rose.

Next to the rose were the words

"marks the spot in Pinkville."

"That must mean we're looking

for a rose that's little and pink!"

I said.

The next day, Molly and I met
at the garden in Pinkville Park.
"The Pinktectives are on the case!"
I said.
"Let's look for clues!"
We searched high and low.

"I see something!" I exclaimed.

"These pink roses are

just like the drawing in our note!"

"Plus, they're little," Molly said.

"Case closed!" I said.

We went over to the gardener.

"We're here for the prize!" I said.

The gardener looked confused.

"Your prize?" she repeated.

"Oh, you must mean
our prized peonies!
They're over here!"

"Our mission is complete!"

I said.

Then I looked at the peonies.

"A flower?" I asked.

"Is that our prize?"

We showed the gardener our note.

"We found your message in a bottle,"

I explained.

"I didn't write that," she said.

"But I do love the stationery!"

"A dead end," Molly said.

"Maybe not," I said.

"Maybe we can find a clue

at the stationery shop."

"Hooray!" Molly said.

"The Pinktectives are on the case."

"Can you tell us anything

about this stationery?"

I asked the shopkeeper.

"It's interesting," he said.

"The paper curls at the edges,

and the ink is fading.

This was written a long time ago."

"If this note is really old,

the prize is probably gone," I said.

"This case is unsolvable!"

Molly and I took a long walk home.
"I guess we'll never find where
the pink rose grows,"
Molly said sadly.
Suddenly I stopped short.
I looked through my binoculars
at a cottage by the sea.
"I spy pinkaperfect roses!" I said.

We hurried over to the cottage.

It was rose-tastic!

Then I spotted something.

"What's this?" I asked.

"Oh my pinkness!" I gasped.

"I can't believe it," Molly said.

"It's the rose from the message!"

"We have to find out more," I said.

"Time to investigate."

In the back of the house,

we found a girl in the garden.

"Hi, I'm Lily!" she said.

We showed Lily the message.

"Did you write this?" Molly asked.

"I didn't," Lily said.

"Not another dead end," I said.

Then I heard someone say, "Oh my!"

"It's my bottle!" said a woman.

"YOU sent this message?" I asked.

"Yes, sixty years ago," she said.

"I'm Rose," she told us.

"I grew up in this house,
and I loved riddles as a kid.

One day I wrote a riddle."

"I threw it out to sea in a bottle.
I couldn't wait to see who would
find it and solve my riddle,
but no one ever did . . . until now!"

"We found the bottle buried
at Pinkville Beach," Molly said.
"The waves must have washed
it back to shore," Rose said.
I can't believe it's been buried
right here in Pinkville all along!"

I thought about Rose's note.

"I solved the riddle!" I exclaimed.

"Little Rose isn't a flower at all—

it's you!

You're little Rose,

and you grew up here!"

"That's correct," Rose said.

"Though I'm not so little anymore!"

"This is pinkamazing," I said.

"Speaking of pink . . . ," Rose said.

She went inside and brought out

two oyster shells.

"You solved my riddle," she said.

"You both deserve your prize!"

We opened our shells.

Inside were perfect pink pearls!

"Thank you!" I said to Rose.

"Now I have something for you, too:

A RIDDLE!"

"What is the best ship in the world?"
I asked.

"Hmmm," Rose said.

"That would have to be *friendship*!"